They were running,
and laughing so hard
that they didn't see the...

Bob the Dog

Written by
Rodrigo
Folgueira

Illustrated by
Poly
Bernatene

First published in 2010
by Meadowside Children's Books
185 Fleet Street, London, EC4A 2HS
www.meadowsidebooks.com

Text © Rodrigo Folgueira
Illustrations © Poly Bernatene
The rights of Rodrigo Folgueira
and Poly Bernatene to be identified
as the author and illustrator
of this work have been asserted
by them in accordance
with the Copyright, Designs
and Patents Act, 1988

A CIP catalogue record for this book
is available from the British Library
10 9 8 7 6 5 4 3 2 1
Printed in China

meadowside 🍃
CHILDREN'S BOOKS

Mark and Bob the Dog
were playing in the park
one day.

GULP!

...tiny little yellow bird.

Bob began to sob.
"Oh, I've eaten him," he cried.
"I've eaten the tiny, innocent,
little **birdy-wirdy**."

Mark tried to comfort him...

...but Bob didn't eat birds.
He sobbed and **wailed** and **howled.**

Then Bob's tummy made a strange noise.

"Tweeeeeet!"

"He's alive, Bob!" cried Mark.

And then a little voice spoke.
"My name is Jeremy.
Jeremy the Canary.
And...

   ...I'm hiding in here!"

And he wouldn't say
another word.

"Oh dear," said Mark. "I think we'd better get some help!"

Bob and Mark gathered
all their friends.

Roger the Rabbit,

Cathy the Cat,

and, of course,
Oscar the Owl.

First, Cathy the Cat tried
blowing pepper up Bob's nose,
to make Jeremy come out
with a sneeze...

ah...ah...
aitchOO!

But that didn't work,
it just made Bob fall over!

Next Roger the Rabbit tried bouncing on Bob's belly to make Jeremy pop out with a burp...

bOing...

bOing...

bOing!

But that didn't work,
it just made Bob feel sick!

Then Oscar the Owl
tried shaking Bob, to make
Jeremy fall out...

whOoah...

arghhh...

blErghh!

But that didn't work either,
it just made Bob feel dizzy!

"Please!"
yelled Mark.
"Somebody help
my dog!"

Suddenly they heard a **deafening** roar.

"J-e-r-e-m-y?!"

bellowed the big canary.

"Mummy?" said Jeremy.

"You'd better
believe it's
Mummy!"
she boomed.

Bob felt a flutter
in his tummy...

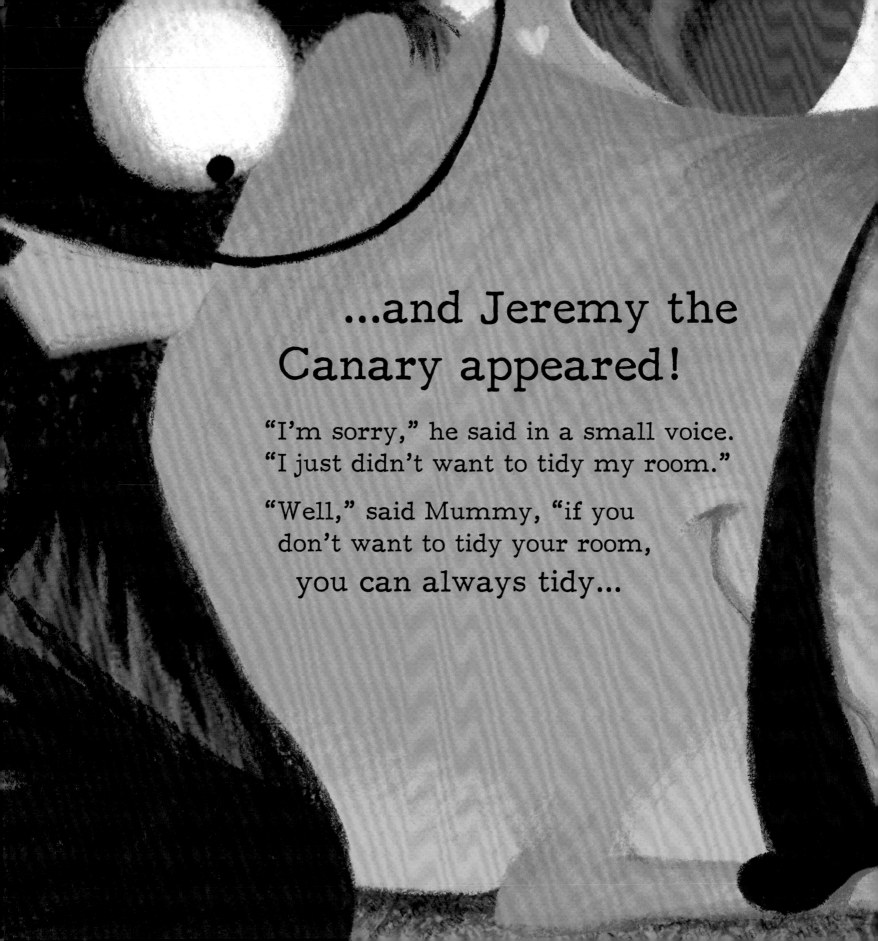

...and Jeremy the Canary appeared!

"I'm sorry," he said in a small voice. "I just didn't want to tidy my room."

"Well," said Mummy, "if you don't want to tidy your room, you can always tidy...

...Bob's room!"

And Jeremy never complained
about tidying his own room,
ever again!